About the Author

Marisa Castronova loves to create. Whether planning fun science lessons, developing new characters, or inventing silly phrases with her children, she loves finding ways to connect with others. With over a decade of teaching experience and a doctorate in education, Marisa is no stranger to the first day of school. In fact, she still reports feeling butterflies in her stomach each and every time a new school year begins. Marisa lives in New Jersey with her husband and two children. When she's not writing or teaching, she can be found soaking up the sun with her family at the beach.

Gigi Feels Jumbled

Addison,

Snuggle up with a
book when you need
it the most!

XO,

M Castronova

Marisa Castronova

Gigi Feels Jumbled

Nightingale Books

NIGHTINGALE PAPERBACK

© Copyright 2021
Marisa Castronova

A CIP catalogue record for this title is
available from the British Library.
ISBN 9781838751463

Nightingale Books is an imprint of
Pegasus Elliot MacKenzie Publishers Ltd.
www.pegasuspublishers.com

First Published in 2021
Nightingale Books
Sheraton House Castle Park
Cambridge England
Printed & Bound in Great Britain

Dedication

For my daughter, Giovanna,
who is always in my heart.

It was the first day of school, I was excited indeed.
"I can't wait to make friends. I can't wait to read."
But on this first day, I also felt scared.
"Will I like my new teacher? Am I really prepared?"

Then all of a sudden, while waiting in line,
I tugged at my mom and let out a cry.
"I don't want to go in! I just want to hide.
I'm feeling anxious and nervous and all jumbled inside."

"Oh dear," said Mom. "Gigi, come close,"
And she gave me a HUG when I needed it most.
"Feeling better?" Mom asked, but I still didn't feel right.
I shook my head no and whimpered, "Not quite."

So once again Mom uttered, "Gigi, come close,"
And she gave me a KISS when I needed it most.
"How about now?" Mom asked, but it still wasn't enough,
All the feelings were still there, I tried to stay tough.

As my eyes started to well, Mom called, "Gigi, come close,"
And she gave me a SNUGGLE when I needed it most.
But alas, no better, still anxious and scared,
Still feeling nervous, not feeling prepared.

But then, Mom smiled, she had the perfect idea,
And a little bit of hope started to appear.
"One HUG – One KISS – One SNUGGLE – won't do!
Gigi, my dear, I have something special for you."

And with that, I got a HUG as tight as could be,
Followed by a KISS, then a SNUGGLE, all three!
"HUGS – KISSES – SNUGGLES!" I said with pride.
"It's the perfect combination when feeling jumbled inside."

And just like magic, all my nerves melted away,
And I finally felt ready for my very first day.
As the school bell rang, the teacher came through the gate.
"Children, line up please! We don't want to be late."
As I turned to dash off, I felt a firm tug,
And Mom softly asked, "Don't I get a hug?"

Looking at Mom's face, I sensed she felt jumbled too.
Mom would miss me terribly wondering how I would do.
So right then and there I whispered, "Mom, come close,"
And I gave her
HUGS – KISSES – SNUGGLES
when she needed it most.

Made in the USA
Columbia, SC
09 September 2021